GW00891734

PUFFIN BOOKS

A Razzle-Dazzle Rainbow

Chris Powling was born in 1943 in London, where he
taught for twenty years in primary and secondary
schools, including ten years as a primary school head-
teacher. He is now Senior Lecturer in English at King
Alfred's College, Winchester, which gives him more time
to write, review, broadcast and generally promote the
notion that bringing children and books happily together
is a thoroughly good thing. Since 1989 he has been
Editor of the children's book magazine *Books For Keeps*.

Shirley McCay.

A Razzle-Dazzle
Rainbow

Chris Powling

Illustrated by
Alan Marks

PUFFIN BOOKS

PUFFIN BOOKS

Published by the Penguin Group
Penguin Books Ltd, 27 Wrights Lane, London W8 5TZ, England
Penguin Books USA Inc., 375 Hudson Street, New York, New York 10014, USA
Penguin Books Australia Ltd, Ringwood, Victoria, Australia
Penguin Books Canada Ltd, 10 Alcorn Avenue, Toronto, Ontario, Canada M4V 3B2
Penguin Books (NZ) Ltd, 182–190 Wairau Road, Auckland 10, New Zealand

Penguin Books Ltd, Registered Offices: Harmondsworth, Middlesex, England

First published by Viking 1993
Published in Puffin Books 1994
1 3 5 7 9 10 8 6 4 2

Text copyright © Chris Powling, 1993
Illustrations copyright © Alan Marks, 1993
All rights reserved

The moral right of the author has been asserted

Printed in England by Clays Ltd, St Ives plc

Except in the United States of America, this book is sold subject
to the condition that it shall not, by way of trade or otherwise, be lent,
re-sold, hired out, or otherwise circulated without the publisher's
prior consent in any form of binding or cover other than that in
which it is published and without a similar condition including this
condition being imposed on the subsequent purchaser

Contents

I
Yen Spends Her Birthday Money

Just a moment.

Are you sure this book is for you?

For a start, it's a daft book, a dickory book, a ding-dong, curly-whirly, cuckoo-boing of a book which couldn't possibly ever be true – not in a million, trillion years.

And for a finish, the kid it really did happen to could easily be your very best friend, assuming you've got one. Don't you think it's a bit . . . well . . . *nosey* to read about your very best friend in a book? How would you like your very best friend to be reading about you?

You wouldn't mind? In that case . . .

Meet Yen.

She was nine years old and she lived in a crumbly, overcrowded bed-and-breakfast hotel in a city so huddled together that everywhere in it seemed to be just around the corner from everywhere else.

Of course, some bed-and-breakfast hotels are lovely. They have sparkly windows, snowy-white steps up to the entrance and a doormat that says VISITORS WELCOME. Yen's hotel wasn't like that at all. It was a damp, dingy place with a doormat that said DROP DEAD – or it would have done if it hadn't been worn so thin it was more like a rag than a rug.

Yen hated it. So did her little brother, Phun. And her big brother Johnny. Also her mum and her dad and Po-Po, her granny. What's more, they weren't the only ones. All the other families in all the other rooms hated it, too: Loi and Anh and Susoi and their parents next door; Lai and Tran with their uncle and aunty upstairs; Michael Kwan plus his granpa down in the basement . . . But why go on? Everyone who lived at the Ajax Hotel hated it so much they could hardly bear to hand over the rent money each week when bossy Mrs Bagbite, who owned the place, came round to collect it.

No wonder Yen was always reading. She reckoned books helped her to forget Mrs Bagbite's hotel. Sometimes, though, even books weren't enough. That's how she felt last Saturday when Phun stopped her on the stairs. 'Where are you off to?' he asked.

'To find my rainbow,' Yen said without thinking.

'Your rainbow?' grinned Phun. 'You mean your rainbow *rope*, don't you? Every kid I know has got one of those.'

'Not a rainbow rope, Phun. I want a *real* rainbow – one that stretches from one side of the sky to the other, showing every colour there is. Because right at the end of it . . .'

'Yes?' said Phun.

'Right at the end of it . . .'

'Go on, Yen.'

But Yen shook her head. How could she tell her little brother what she'd read in the story?

Would she really find a pot of gold where her rainbow touched the ground?

Of course not!

Serve her right if Phun laughed at her. Why, with a pot of gold you could buy anything you wanted – a proper house, for instance, out at the city limits where the country began and her family would live happily ever after. But who could possibly believe in that? 'Never mind, Phun,' Yen sighed. 'I'm just dreaming.'

'Why don't you buy one?' Phun suggested.

'A rainbow?'

'A rainbow *rope*, dimbo. Now you've got your birthday money maybe you can afford one.'

'Oh . . . I see what you mean,' Yen nodded.

All summer long, rainbow ropes had been the city's Latest Craze. Everywhere you went you could see kids dipping them, flipping them, skipping them, tripping them, whipping them and zipping them in a dazzle of colour that went right round the clock because rainbow ropes glowed in the daylight as well as the dark. Some kids even *wore* a rainbow rope if they wanted to look extra fancy. 'You're right, Phun,' said Yen. 'That's what I'll buy with my birthday money – a rainbow rope!' And she set off at once to find one.

Yen tried everywhere: the big stores in the city centre with their uppity assistants and ultra-smooth escalators; the fly-by-night stalls in the market which sold something different every day; even the tatty old warehouse opposite the bus station with its piles and piles of kids stuff. 'A rainbow rope?' each one answered. 'Sorry, dear. We've run out of those. So has everybody else, probably.'

By mid-afternoon, Yen was ready to give up. 'Besides,' she told herself, 'this is the only place left, just about. And it's as scruffy as the Ajax Hotel.'

She was talking about a shop just ahead of

her, half-hidden by a railway arch, in the oldest part of the city.

If it was a shop, that is.

It was more like a lock-up, really. Or an overgrown tool-shed. 'What a dump,' Yen sniffed.

Straight away, she wished she hadn't. The shop or shed or lock-up *smelled* like the Ajax Hotel, too. Yen wrinkled her nose as she pushed open the door and looked inside. 'Mister?' she called.

'Who's that?' The man stooping over the work-bench in the corner swung round so fast he made Yen jump. 'What do you want?' he demanded.

'Only a rainbow rope, mister.'

'A rainbow rope?'

Yen felt sharp, crafty eyes looking her over from her skimpy anorak and worn-out jeans down to her tatty trainers. 'I thought you might sell them, mister,' she said hastily. 'I can see you don't, though – not with all this equipment and stuff lying about. I'm really sorry I bothered you.'

'A rainbow rope did you say?'

'To buy with my birthday money, mister. But I realize this isn't a toyshop –'

'Wait, kid.'

The shopkeeper – if that's what he was – had whiskery ears, a head as bald as a bollard and the kind of smile that told Yen at once he didn't like children very much. When he spoke, though, his voice was almost smarmy. He sounded like a crocodile trying to con her into a kiss. 'Er . . . let's suppose I *have* got a rainbow rope, kid. If I sold it to you, what would you do with it?'

'Do with it?' said Yen in surprise. 'I'd do what all the kids do, mister. Only more so because I've waited so long for mine. I'd dip it and flip it and skip it and trip it and whip it and –'

'That's fine, kid, fine. So . . . it's rather a special rope you're looking for, is it? An out-of-the-ordinary rope? A *heavy-duty* rope, you might say?'

'Well, yes . . .' said Yen. 'If you've got one I can afford.'

'Kid, this is your lucky day.' Already he was bending down behind the work-bench.

Shifty-shifty went some boxes.

Clickety-clack went a key in a lock.

Creako-creako-creako went the steel door of a safe as it swung open.

All this for a rainbow rope?

As the sort-of shopkeeper stood up, Yen took a hasty step backwards. Partly she was nervous about the way he was holding the rope – as if half-expecting it to bite his bum at any moment – and partly she was amazed by the rope itself.

Out-of-the-ordinary, was it?

You can bet on that.

This was the most rainbow-like rope or maybe the ropiest rainbow, Yen had ever seen in her life. It shimmered and shone in front of her like a coil of colour so blinding you needed dark glasses to see the best of it. 'It's brilliant!' Yen gasped. 'Truly brilliant! How much is it, though?'

'How much have you got?'

Yen's face fell. 'Fifty pence,' she said.

'That's all?'

'Sorry, mister . . .'

The man's teeth flashed in a smile as glinty as the top of his head. 'No need to be sorry, kid. Fifty pence happens to be the price of this rope.'

'Fifty pence?' Yen gasped. 'For a rainbow rope as wonderful as this?'

'Fifty pence, kid. That is . . . provided you make me a promise.'

'A promise, mister?'

'You must promise to give this rope plenty of

exercise. It isn't a rope you can stash at the back of your toy-cupboard and forget about, you know. This rope must be played with – really played with. For day after day after day. Even if you *do* get fed up with it.'

'Fed up with it?' Yen blinked. 'Who could possibly get fed up with such a magical rope? It's like . . . Technicolored lightning!'

'So you promise to take good care of it?'

'Of course I will.'

'It's yours, then.'

Quick as a conjuring trick, he'd snatched her fifty pence, slapped the rainbow rope round her neck and hustled Yen out on to the pavement. 'Cheerio, kid,' he snapped. 'Don't forget, make that rope work. Make it *sweat*. Keep on keeping on with it till . . . till . . . till you've had every pennyworth of your birthday money.'

'You can count on that, mister. And thanks very much. You've been ever so –'

Too late.

He'd slammed the door shut so hard it was as if he were glad to see the back of her.

Or was it the rope he couldn't stand?

Surely not the rope . . .

Yen shrugged. Why should she worry if for once in her life someone had done her a favour?

'What a weirdo he was, though!' she exclaimed. 'Not like a proper shopkeeper at all.'

Nod-nod-nod.

One end of the rainbow rope seemed to be agreeing with her. It swayed up and down in the breeze like a snake saying yes to its supper.

Yen felt a shiver run up and down her spine. And no one can blame her for that. For here comes the very first daft, dickory, ding-dong, curly-whirly, cuckoo-boing bit of the story.

HOW COULD THE RAINBOW ROPE BE SWAYING IN THE BREEZE WHEN THERE WASN'T A BREATH OF WIND ANYWHERE IN THE CITY?

2
Sword Play

'Stoppit!' Yen told herself. 'You're imagining things again. It's all those story-books you read. They're turning your brain into bric-à-brac.'

She wasn't sure what bric-à-brac was but she'd seen the words used at a Boot Fair so she knew they meant something junky.

The rainbow rope stayed still.

It hung round her neck like superstretch spaghetti fresh out of the saucepan – except spaghetti doesn't have a star-shiny glitter to it and glimmer through all the shades of the spectrum as you look. 'It's amazing,' Yen said.

So it was.

Surely, no kid in the world had ever got more for her birthday money than Yen! Wasn't it the best fifty pence she'd ever spent? Of course, it was also the *only* fifty pence she'd ever spent – on herself at any rate – but this didn't lower her opinion of the rainbow rope. 'It's splendificent!' she crowed. 'It's fantabulous! It's magnastic!'

Suddenly, the drab autumn half-term felt as frisky as springtime.

Yen, too.

As she skipped along the pavement, she heard the rainbow rope bounce up and down round her shoulders with a sound somewhere between a burp and a whisper. 'Stick with me, rope,' Yen called. 'You and me, we're chums! We're mates! We're pals! We're partners! We're make-up, make-up, never-never-break-up *buddies*, that's what we are!'

Yen was so happy she didn't really look where she was going.

Maybe that's why she took the wrong turning back through the railway arch.

At first she didn't notice how the streets all around got more and more narrow, more and more mean. It was as if the hungriest part of the city lay in wait for her, licking its lips. Soon every doorway she passed was like a trap ready to be sprung and every broken window – with its jagged see-through teeth – was like a mouth, eager to bite.

Yen stopped by a crooked lamp-post. 'I'm lost,' she wailed. 'Where is everybody?'

Because she knew people were there.

Would someone slide out of that old dustbin opposite? Or sneak over this spiky-topped wall? Who was skulking behind those mouldy sacks strung out between the houses? 'Oo-er,' Yen whimpered. 'I don't like it here . . .'

'She's got a rainbow rope,' came a hoarse, hard voice close by. 'Cost money, they do.'

'Big money,' another voice joined in.

'We could do with some big money,' added a third voice. 'Couldn't we?'

'Big, small or medium,' the first voice answered. 'Who cares so long as it's money?'

'Yeah, who cares?'

'Shall we splatter her, then?'

'Why not?'

Yen nearly fainted from fright.

Then, quite suddenly, came the second bit of this story that's so daft, so dickory, so ding-dong, curly-whirly, cuckoo-boingish, you'd better lie down at once with an ice-pack on your head if you're tempted to believe it.

You see, the rainbow rope – yes, all on its own – unwound itself from Yen's neck, went as stiff as a poker, sharp as a razor, pointy as a park-keeper's litter-stick and fitted itself in Yen's fist so snugly it was like a sword forged especially for her. 'A sword?' Yen yelped.

For that's what she'd got: a snickersnack

sword so vorpal it could have chopped off the head of a Jabberwock, no sweat.

Nervously, Yen swished it around her. What a shame the lamp-post got in the way . . . for the sword sliced through it like a bread knife through blancmange.

ZIP!

Was the top half of the lamp-post really teetering on the bottom half?

CLONK-CLATTER-TINKLE!

Yen gaped at the wreckage all round her, partly sticking up, partly lying flat and partly smashed-to-smithereens across the pavement. 'Was that my fault?' she exclaimed.

Behind her, she heard three pairs of feet fading into the distance. 'Hey,' Yen called, 'I didn't do it on purpose. Oops! I mean, *of course* I did it on purpose! And if I hear any more talk about splattering me and stealing my rope I'll slit you from your guzzle to your snatch, whoever you are.'

She liked the sound of that – it came from a story her best-ever teacher had once read in class.

Yen liked the look of her sword as well. But she was careful how she whisked it about as she hurried back the way she'd come. After all, suppose she snipped another lamp-post in two? Or diced up a dustbin with someone hiding inside? Or separated one side of the railway arch from the other so the next train to cross it toppled smack on its buffers in the road?

The railway arch, did I say?

Yen gave a shout of relief. For there, in front of her was the railway arch along with the turning she should have taken in the first place. 'Thanks, rainbow rope,' she said. 'It was really tricky back there. I don't know what I'd have done without you.'

The rainbow rope said nothing. It simply wound itself round and round her arm in a hundred eye-catching coils, yet so lightly Yen scarcely felt the weight of it. 'And thank you, Mr Shopkeeper,' she waved. 'This is the best rainbow rope in the universe! Why, it's as good as an actual rainbow!'

Except for the pot of gold, of course. Yen had forgotten that. She was so bewitched by her birthday present she couldn't imagine how it could be better . . .

But somebody could.

From the shadows beyond the railway arch, this somebody had been watching Yen and her rope for quite a while now.

Who was it?

And why was this person so eager not to be seen?

Behind her, always behind her – leaving a big enough gap to make quite, quite sure she didn't notice – this slinking, sidling somebody followed Yen every step of the way back to the Ajax Hotel.

3
Bow and Arrow

Where could Yen keep her rainbow rope?

Under her bed? No, because she slept on the floor – on a mattress tight up against the sink and the fridge.

In the cupboard by the stove? No, because that's where she and Phun and Johnny hung up their clothes.

Next to the laundry basket behind the door? No, because Phun stored his computer there – his special computer which he'd won in a Christmas competition two years before when a local newspaper had called him 'a five-year-old mathematical genius'.

On the shelf above the armchairs, then? Wrong, again. Wasn't that where the crockery, cutlery and cooking stuff was stacked? Also Johnny had already bagged the space beneath the dining-table for his tool-kit which – one day, when he could afford the time for evening classes – would help him become a car mechanic instead

of a waiter. Poor Johnny! He worked so hard, and spent so much of his wages on the family, Yen couldn't bear to disturb him.

The tiny room across the corridor was no good, either. Dad and Mum and Granny Po-Po slept here – so hugger-muggerly they had to take it in turns to snore, Dad joked. As soon as he was well enough to find a job himself the whole family would move somewhere better . . .

Yen sighed. Her dad was so ill he looked older than Granny Po-Po these days. Would he ever get well again in the Ajax Hotel – especially meeting Mrs Bagbite week after week?

Still, at least she had a rainbow rope now. 'I can always sleep with it under my pillow,' she said.

'All of it?' Phun asked. 'Won't a lot of it spill out on the floor? It's the longest rainbow rope I've ever seen.'

'Sometimes it is,' said Yen. 'Not always, though. It can change its size and shape, this rainbow rope.'

'You reckon?'

'I do, yes.'

She knew he didn't believe her. Phun thought she was being story-bookish again. That's why she didn't dare tell him the rope was swordlike

as well. If she hadn't seen it with her own eyes
she wouldn't have believed it herself.

If she did believe it . . .

Could it all have been a dream, she wondered?
She had to admit that made sense. 'I scared
myself silly, I expect. I got myself in such a tizz
I went all daft and dickory and ding-dong,
curly-whirly, cuckoo-boingable. OK, so it was a
sword I saw. But couldn't it just as easily have
been a ghost or a goblin? Honestly, Yen! That
rope will transform itself into the Frumious
Bandersnatch next, according to you. What you
need is a good kick in the pants.'

She was so cross she paid herself out by refusing to play with her new toy – even though that's what she wanted to do more than anything.

Well, almost anything.

Yen still loved reading best of all. Propped up on top of the fridge was her private library – the four books she looked at most often because each one was a present from her mum and her dad. Her Favourite Four she called them:

Through the Looking-Glass by Lewis Carroll.
The Iron Man by Ted Hughes.
The BFG by Roald Dahl.
The Sky in the Pie by Roger McGough.

She shut her eyes and picked one at random, letting it fall open at any page it liked.

Eeek!

They weren't the words she'd have chosen –
not so soon after her adventure under the
railway arch. But she spoke them aloud,
anyway:

> And, as in uffish thought he stood,
>   The Jabberwock with eyes of flame,
> Came whiffling through the tulgey wood,
>   And burbled as it came!

After this, Yen recited the whole poem till every
square centimetre of the kitchen-cum-bedroom-
cum-sitting-room seemed to glow with the thrill
of it.

Wait, though.

Was it the poem or the rope which lit up the tulginess? 'Whatever's the matter?' Yen asked. 'Are you tying yourself in a knot?'

For the rainbow rope was all-of-a-fidget. It crackled and fizzed like a firework display. Was it burbling? Was it whiffling? Was it uffish?

It was over-excited, that's for sure. 'Good job I dumped you in the sink,' said Yen. 'You're as jumpy as a frisbee with frost-bite!'

Thank goodness Johnny was out at work and Mum and Dad and Phun and Granny Po-Po were in the other room watching television. 'If they saw you now,' Yen remarked, 'they'd never let me keep you indoors. Can't you cool it, rainbow rope?'

To her relief, the rope tucked itself under the taps and settled down. All she could hear was a sound somewhere between a whisper and a burp.

She could still hear it long after bedtime with Phun spark out beside her and Johnny so tired he hadn't even said 'sleep tight' after he got undressed in the dark. 'Send him a nice dream, BFG,' yawned Yen. 'About evening classes, for instance . . . or being a car mechanic. And don't forget Phun, or Granny Po-Po, or Mum and Dad. They'd like some scrumdiddlyumptious dreams as well if it's all right with you. Nothing troggle-humpish, please.'

As usual, her own dreams took her out to the city limits where the country began.

Soon the Ajax Hotel was silent. Only the drip-drip-drip of a leaky cistern could be heard along with the squeak-squeak-squeak of someone easing open a window.

Easing open a window?

Slowly, staying as quiet as she could, Yen sat up. Yes, the window was definitely open. She could feel an after-dark breeze on her cheeks and see the curtains pulled back on a skyful of stars. Had the rainbow rope done that? For there it was, stretched across the gap, its colours silvery in the moonlight. What was it up to?

First, it made the shape of a D fallen flat on its back like this:

Then it added a V like this:

Last, it split the V and the D with an I like this:

Yen watched in astonishment as the V bit pulled the I bit across the D bit just the way you pull an arrow across a bow. 'OK, so you're fed up with being a sword,' she said. 'Now you're a bow and arrow. But what are you shooting at, rainbow rope – the moon?'

By now the bow was fully bent.

Yen held her breath.

THWOP!

The rainbow rope flipped back on itself like a piece of snapped elastic or a catapult that's lost its stone. For a moment it seemed to be resting. Then it tried again.

THWOP!

And again.

THWOP!

After this it lay beneath the window in a worn-out, moonlighty tangle.

Quickly, Yen pushed back the bedclothes. Kneeling close to the rope so she wouldn't wake Phun or Johnny, she said 'Didn't you realize what would happen, rainbow rope? A bow can't shoot an arrow by itself, you know, especially when the two are all-of-a-piece.'

The rainbow rope didn't move.

Yen sighed and stood up. She'd better shut the window or they'd all have a shivery night.

But where was the rainbow rope aiming?

She leaned over the sill to sniff the night air. 'I feel like Sophie staring out of her bedroom at the orphanage,' she said. 'I can't see the Big Friendly Giant coming down the street, though.'

Actually, she couldn't see anything coming

down the street. It was much too late now even for burglars unless they were the sort of daft, dickory, ding-dong, cuckoo-boing type burglars who didn't care if it was nearly dawn. Or like that curly-whirly clot in the shadows below who seemed to be waiting for the last bus. Wasn't it obvious he must've missed it? 'Maybe he's early for the first bus,' Yen yawned. 'Good luck to him because he'll have to wait for ages . . . for ages . . .'

Her voice trailed away as she heard what she'd said.

What first bus?

What last bus, come to that?'

The bus company had stopped its service to this part of the city weeks ago – not enough money to be made, they reckoned. That's why they'd put a criss-cross of glo-tape over the bus-stop sign where everyone could see it even at night. 'He must be *pretending* to wait for a bus,' Yen said. 'Why would anyone do that? How funny!'

And she was right, of course.

The mystery mister staring up at her window *was* funny in a way – assuming, that is, Yen meant funny 'peculiar' rather than funny 'ha-ha'.

4
Rope Tricks

When Yen checked the bus-stop next
morning, no one was there. 'Maybe what I saw
was just a trick of the light – or one of those
mirage things they get in the desert,' she told
herself.

'What?' said Phun, sleepily.

'Nothing,' said Yen.

Already she was busy with breakfast.

She washed up afterwards, as well, and shook
out all the bedding while the rest of the family
got dressed. So even Granny Po-Po couldn't
complain when she told them she was going out.
'Only to the park,' Yen explained. 'To try out
my new rainbow rope. Want to come, Phun?'

'Maybe tomorrow,' he said. 'Today I'm
playing with my computer.'

'Fine,' said Yen as she left.

Till she knew her rope a bit better, she
preferred to be on her own. Mind you, it was as
good-as-gold right now. Twinkling in the

Sunday sunshine, it hung over her arm like a
lassoo on loan from some multicoloured cowboy.

Yen loved the local park.

It wasn't very big – just enough grass to puff
a kid out, in fact – but up there on top of the
hill, with a clear, blue sky overhead and leaves
skittering around her feet, Yen felt it was
downright city limit like.

Pity it was almost empty . . .

Had she got there too early? Yen gazed
around her in dismay. 'What, no rainbow ropes
here except mine? Has the Craze finished
already – just when I'm able to join in?'

Apart from a few footballers over by the

changing hut, she was all alone. 'Hi, Yen!' called one of them.

'Hi, Bash!' answered Yen.

She perked up at once. Bashir was captain of the school football team so it was a big compliment if he even noticed you. 'Aren't you watching the Autumn Parade, Yen?' he asked, coming over.

'Parade?'

'In the High Street.'

'So that's where everyone is! I forgot, Bash.'

'We didn't. We just prefer football. Right, team?'

'Right, Bash,' grinned the others.

'Which is why we like those terrific goal-posts of yours, Yen. Never seen anything like them – not even at Wembley Stadium. Luminous, aren't they?'

'Luminous?' said Yen, turning round. 'Oh . . . *those* goal-posts.'

For there stood the rainbow rope, stiffly to attention, in a goal-shaped outline so dazzling you could have seen it in a pitch-black stadium without switching on a single floodlight.

The footballers couldn't believe their luck. 'Er . . . fancy a game, Yen?' Bash suggested. 'Using your goal-posts? We could play all-against-all if you like.'

'Me?' Yen said.

She looked down at her scruffy trainers. 'OK, Bash. If you think I'm good enough.'

Good enough?

Within seconds Yen scored her first goal. 'Hooray!' cheered Bash.

Goal number two came a minute later. 'Hooray . . .' said Bash less cheerfully.

When goal number three and goal number four quickly followed he wasn't cheerful at all. 'Hoo-flippin'-ray,' he scowled. 'Yen, I know it's a bit windy today but how come these goal-posts of yours always sway *away* from the ball

when we shoot but *towards* the ball when you
shoot?'

'No idea,' Yen swallowed.

'Reckon we'll just have to play a bit harder,
then.'

'Er . . . reckon so, Bash.'

So they did.

They blocked Yen with sliding-tackles, close-
marking and the off-side trap. They beat her
with dribbles, dummies and the occasional
banana shot. They bamboozled her with every
dead-ball set-up they'd ever practised . . . and
none of it made a scrap of difference.

Soon Yen was six nil in the lead.

Then eight nil.

Her tenth goal was the finish of it. Scooping away Bash's near-post header at the very last moment, the rainbow rope flicked the ball at Yen, who happened to be facing the wrong way and let the ball rebound from her bottom back across the goal-line.

Bash was sick as a parrot.

'We wuz robbed!' he roared. 'Yen, I don't know how you're working them but you can stuff those ponky, bendy goal-posts. I've had enough!'

'It's not me, Bash,' Yen wailed.

'Isn't it?'

'No!'

She was so upset they almost believed her . . . till they saw how the rope shook with whispery, burp-like giggles. 'Stoppit!' Yen begged.

Too late.

Who could blame Bash and the others for snatching up the football and storming off in a huff?

Miserably, Yen stuffed the rainbow rope under her anorak. 'Thanks a bunch, rope,' she said. 'Now the whole school will think I don't play fair. You've really put me in a mood. I'd better go home the long way till I get over it.'

The long way took Yen through the most
respectable part of the city – down streets so
quiet and tidy she was convinced every house
must belong to a teacher. 'Probably they're all
indoors doing their half-term marking . . .'

She was gazing at a neat, freshly painted
bungalow as she said this. It was just the sort of
home she dreamed about. 'So kindly behave
yourself, rope,' she grumbled. 'You've done
enough damage for today.'

Of course, it was a silly thing to say.

Already she felt the rope worming its way down the sleeve of her anorak. It flopped on to the pavement, slipped through the picket fence and shimmied across the bungalow's trim, green lawn. 'Oh, no,' gasped Yen. 'Not the garden gnome . . .'

The gnome was standing on the far side of a small, ornamental pond. Yen watched in horror as the rope slid into the water and loopy-looped towards it like a skinny Loch Ness monster.

Dum-dum! Dum-dum! Dum-dum! Dum-dum!

KERPLONK!

The gnome's nose and toes and bulging belly in between stuck up like sharks' fins as the rainbow rope towed it backwards and forwards across the pond in a frenzy of racing turns. 'Do you MIND!' came a shout from the house. 'That snake of yours is drowning my gnome!'

'It's not a snake, Mrs,' Yen tried to explain. 'It's my new rainbow rope, I'm afraid.'

'A rainbow rope? Attacking a garden gnome in broad daylight? You must think I'm *stupid*, you little hooligan!'

The lady had the sort of voice which would have made every kid in the world sit up straight in assembly.

She didn't impress Yen's rope, though.

With a flick of its tail – or maybe its head – it reared itself out of the water and tossed the garden gnome straight through the open window where the lady was standing.

THUMP!

Before the sound of gnome-nobbled lady had died away, the rope's giggles had taken over. It snuffled and wuffled on the side of the pond as if in the grip of the Phantom Tickler. 'That's supposed to be *funny*?' the lady shrieked.

Yen ran, of course.

She knew she should have stayed to say sorry but what would you have done? By the time she reached the High Street she was panting so much she could hardly speak. 'OK, so I've wasted my fifty pence. Good riddance, I say.'

'Want to go to the front, kid?' someone asked.

'The front?' said Yen.

'Down by the kerb – to see the Parade.'

'Oh . . . yes. Thanks, mister.' *That's* why the pavement was so crowded!

Eagerly, Yen elbowed her way forward. The Autumn Parade was just what she needed to take her mind off the rainbow rope. Could she hear the band already?

No, not yet.

She felt excitement bubbling inside. All round her, people stood on tiptoe, craning their necks.

Was *that* the band, then?

Another false alarm!

Or that?

YES!

Suddenly, it arrived – Left-right! Left-right! Left-right! – swinging round the corner in such swanky, razzamatazzy, high-stepping style Yen found herself marching on the spot the way she did every year. Soon pipes, trumpets and xylophones were root-tooting past her – followed by the rattle of side drums and the BOM! BOM! BOM! of the big drum. 'How do they stay together?' a little kid squeaked.

'The girl out in front,' said Yen. 'She's called the drum major and she beats time with that long, glittery stick she's throwing up in the air . . . that long glittery . . .'

Stick?

Not any more.

Yen never found out how the rope had swopped itself for the drum major's baton. Nor did she see what happened next because she shut her eyes tight. That way she only *heard* the catastrophe.

**BOOM-DIDDY-WALLOP-THUD-BANG-ZAP-POW!
TARAN-TARA-TARAN TA –
ZONK!**

Hee-haw! Hee-haw! Hee-haw!

Before the police cars arrived to cope with the commotion, Yen was off again – in a helter-skelter sprint so panicky it was as if Mrs Bagbite in person were hotfooting after her. No rainbow rope, however streamlined and supersonic, could possibly have kept up as she hurtled through alleyways, round corners, along roads, over a bridge or two and finally down the hill to the Ajax Hotel. 'I'm mega-mangled,' she choked.

'Nuclear-knackered, that's me. But at least
I've got away from that daft, dickory, ding-
dong, curly-whirly, cuckoo-boingastic *rope*. OK,
so I've broken my promise to the shopkeeper. It
can fend for itself from now on. See if I care!'

The trouble was Yen did care.

She couldn't help it. The present she'd bought
with her birthday money may have been a
cheating, vandalizing, rumbustious all-round
wrecker-of-a-rope but it was extra-special,
wasn't it?

Hadn't she fled from something strange and
wonderful?

Maybe that's why she didn't scream out loud
as she dragged herself up the Hotel steps and
her eyes drew level with the raggedy doormat.

For there in front of her, snuggled up in its own coils like a collapsed laundry basket, was the rainbow rope.

Yen grinned with relief.

She wasn't the only one.

On the other side of the street, huddled behind a broken-down billboard, someone else was grinning too. With a face sticky from sweat and a chest heaving for breath, Yen's minder – if that's the right word – had kept up with each one of the rope's tricks. Everything, so far, was going strictly according to plan . . .

5

The Favourite Four

'It's simple, Yen,' Phun told her.

'Is it?'

'You went *through* the back-alleys, right? And *round* the corners, *along* the roads, *over* the bridges, *down* the hill . . .'

'So?'

'A rainbow rope needn't do that. It can take a short-cut *across* everything. Probably it only had to cover half the distance you did. For all we know it might've dived underground and popped up out of a drain opposite the Ajax Hotel.'

'Oh . . .'

Yen glanced at the sink. It was brimful of rainbow rope from taps to plughole. 'Maybe that's why it looked a bit smudgy,' she said.

'Exactly.'

Phun was thinking hard. 'And you're not kidding me, Yen? About the sword, I mean? And the bow and arrow?'

'I'm not kidding you about the goal-posts, either. Or the garden gnome. And I bet we see what happened to the Autumn Parade on the Six o'Clock News. Honestly, Phun, I was so *embarrassed*. I suppose I should've expected it, really – considering how twitchy that shopkeeper was when he handed the rope over. He seemed to be terrified it might duff him up on the spot.'

'Tyrannosaurus Rope, huh?'

'More like a razzle-dazzle rope if you ask me,' said Yen. 'I'll never dare show my face in the park again. Not to mention the High Street and that road where the lady lives.'

'Oh, I shouldn't worry, Yen. Most likely they hardly saw you. They'd have been too busy gawping at the rope.'

'How about Bash?'

'Bash?' Phun grinned. 'I bet he's sworn the others to secrecy. I mean, losing ten-nil to someone who's not even in the school football team? Just because of dodgy goal-posts? Not very convincing, is it! He'd die of shame if it ever got out.'

'I suppose so,' Yen nodded.

She always felt better when she shared her worries with Phun. Wasn't he the best little brother in the world?

Clever, too.

Even now she could see him turning something over in his mind. 'If only it could speak to you,' he said.

'The rope?' said Yen.

'Why not? It understands everything *you* say, doesn't it? So how can you find out what *it's* got to say?'

'Impossible!'

'Not if you teach it to write . . .'

'To write?'

'By shaping itself into words, Yen. According to you it can make a D and a V and a C already – when it turns itself into a bow and arrow. And what about the sword? Isn't that a kind of T? Don't forget those goal-posts, either. If the crossbar dips a bit, you've got an M, haven't you? And isn't a drum major's stick close to a capital I? That's six letters before you've begun. Only twenty more to go! Mind you, they've got to be put into words people can recognize . . . which means you've got to teach the rope to read, come to think of it. Don't reading and writing go together? You've got everything you need right here in this room.'

'Have I?'

'Those books of yours, Yen: your Favourite Four. Why don't you start the rope off with a story? Or maybe some poems? I reckon a rope as bright as this one will soon get the hang of it.'

'Like Miss Davis did with me?' Yen said.

'And me,' said Phun.

Suddenly the day felt frabjous after all.

Teaching the rainbow rope to read and write?

Yen couldn't imagine anything so outstandingly daft, dickory, ding-dong, curly-whirly, cuckoo-boingacious! Hadn't she always wanted to be like Miss Davis, her best-ever teacher? 'Books are magical,' Miss Davis always said. 'If you let them, they'll cast a spell on you.'

Was Yen as good a teacher as Miss Davis, though?

Nervously, she waited till the tappety-tap of Phun on his computer told her he wouldn't be listening. Then she lifted the rainbow rope from the sink, draped it across her lap and began to read.

Poetry first.

She chose her special poem – the one she read

to Johnny when she wanted to cheer him up after a bad day. 'It's by Roger McGough,' she announced. 'You'll love it, rope. It's really funny.'

Waiter, there's a sky in my pie
Remove it at once if you please
You can keep your incredible sunsets
I ordered mincemeat and cheese

I can't stand nightingales singing
Or clouds all burnished with gold
The whispering breeze is disturbing the peas
And making my chips go all cold

I don't care if the chef is an artist
Whose canvases hang in the Tate
I want two veg. and puff pastry
Not the Universe heaped on my plate

Yen turned the page. 'What do you think of it so far, rope?' she asked. No answer – not even 'Rubbish!' Yen shrugged and went on:

OK I'll try just a spoonful
I suppose I've got nothing to lose
Mm . . . the colours quite tickle the palette
With a blend of delicate hues

She broke off, giggling. 'That's a joke,' she explained. 'He should have written "palate", you see – spelled P-A-L-A-T-E which is a bit of your mouth you taste with. He wrote "palette" instead – spelled P-A-L-E-T-T-E because that's what an artist mixes his paints on. Isn't that clever?'

The rainbow didn't move.

Yen bit her lip. 'Sorry, rope,' she said. 'I forgot one of Miss Davis's strictest rules. I should have read the poem straight through before we started talking about it – otherwise it gets all bits-and-piecey. I won't interrupt again, I promise.'

> The sun has a custardy flavour
> And the clouds are as light as air
> And the wind a chewier texture
> (With a hint of cinnamon there?)

This sky is simply delicious
Why haven't I tried it before?
I can chew my way through to Eternity
And still have room left for more

Having acquired a taste for the Cosmos
I'll polish this sunset off soon
I can't wait to tuck into the night sky
Waiter! Please bring me the Moon!

The last line was Johnny's favourite. However weary he was when he got home from work, it always made him laugh out loud. Would it tickle the rainbow rope's fancy?

Not that Yen could see.

Apart from a glint or two, the rope looked so ordinary it could have come from the Games Trolley at school. 'Maybe Phun got it wrong for once,' Yen said.

But he hadn't.

Slowly, almost shyly, one end of the rope sneaked out of Yen's lap, edged up the spine of the book . . . and flipped back the page. 'Again?' Yen said. 'You want the poem again?'

Over and over again!

The rope wouldn't let Yen stop – barely for breath never mind for a breather. Even a trip to the loo was out of the question. 'Don't you

know the poem by heart yet?' she protested.
'Honestly, I know it by *hurt* practically. I've
never had such a sore throat!'

Yen smiled as she said it, though.

Especially later on when the rope wrote its
first word . . .

Of course, it was mostly copying. But wasn't that
amazing enough? 'Look, Phun,' Yen gulped.

'Sky?' said Phun, swinging round.

He'd read the word at once despite the rope's
wobbliness as it balanced itself on its two ends.

'Try shutting the book,' Phun suggested. 'Let it write the word on its own.'

The rope froze. It looked like an enormous twisty-turny icicle. 'Go for it!' coaxed Yen.

So the rope did. Not as fast as before, admittedly . . .

'Sky!' whooped Phun and Yen.

They hugged each other with delight. They'd have hugged the rope, too, if it hadn't switched to a different outline. 'What's it doing now?' Phun asked. 'Some kind of kite?'

'A pointer,' said Yen. 'A shaky pointer. But what's it pointing *at*? The window, is it?'

As they turned to look, their mouths dropped open.

No wonder the rope was shaky.

Was it the Bloodbottler they saw? Or the Gizzardgulper? Or the Fleshlumpeater himself?

Not quite . . .

Tall as he was, the hooded figure on top of the ladder propped against their sill wasn't quite gigantic enough to have come from the pages of *The BFG*. How long had he been there, though? And why was he peering in at them? 'Is it a window-cleaner?' Yen swallowed.

'At the Ajax Hotel?' snorted Phun. 'Besides, where's his bucket and sponge? If only we could see him properly through that gungy glass . . .'

'Speak for yourself, Phun!'

'Yen, he's going.'

'Good!'

But even as the frightsome shape at the window dropped rung by rung out of sight, Yen knew she'd see it again. She also knew – deep down in some daft, dickory, ding-dong, curly-whirly, cuckoo-boingarchic part of her brain that was just out of reach – she'd seen it somewhere before.

6

Rent Day

Yen and Phun were ready now.

Their eyes darted everywhere. After this,
though, there wasn't a trace of the Peeping Tom.

Unless, that is, the flash of light from the roof-
tops opposite was the sun glinting on binoculars.
And how could they explain the deafening
dustbin-liddery clatter they heard long after
dark out in the Hotel's backyard?

Just the wind?

Really?

Of course, they couldn't be sure. 'I haven't a clue what's going on,' Yen groaned next morning. 'Why was the rope trying so hard to upset me the other day – as if I wasn't allowed to get too fond of it? And was it really trying to fly out of the window the night before? And now, for goodness' sake, we've got a spy to worry about! Honestly, Phun, I feel about as safe as a mouse in a cat basket. How am I supposed to concentrate on teaching it to read and write?'

'It's the rope that needs to concentrate,' Phun pointed out.

The trouble was, the rope had the jitters too. How else could Yen explain its sudden backflips in the air as if to startle someone behind it? 'Are you scared as well, rope?' Yen asked. 'Is that why we're not making any progress?'

The rope seemed to droop in despair.

. . . it spelled out. Then again . . .

'I know,' Yen nodded. 'That's "sky". You learnt
it ages ago. How about a new word, rope?'

'Maybe you're rushing things,' said Phun.
'Learning to read and write isn't like
programming a computer, Yen.'

Yen shook her head. 'Something's wrong,

Phun. I'm convinced of it.'

'Give it some *Iron Man*,' Phun suggested.

At this, the rope stiffened.

Of all Yen's books *The Iron Man* was the one it liked best. It acted out every scene as she went along – from bunching up like the Iron Man's fist to flopping flat like the space-bat-angel-dragon crashlanding on Australia. 'OK, rainbow rope,' said Yen. '*Iron Man* it is. Where shall I start?'

wrote the rope at once.

'Bor-*ing*,' Yen said

She didn't mean the story. She meant reciting the same passage for the umpteenth time – the lines the rope always wanted:

One of the stars of the night sky had begun to change. This star had always been a very tiny star, of no importance at all . . .

As Yen read on, describing how the star grew bigger and Bigger and BIGger and BIGGER because it hurtled nearer and Nearer and NEARer and NEARER to the earth, the rope seemed to hold its breath till she reached the climax:

> . . . if it hit the world at that speed, why, the whole world would simply be blasted to bits in the twinkling of an eye. It would be like an express train hitting a bowl of goldfish.

Wow!

Without fail, the rope went limp with excitement.

Yen, too.

Maybe Miss Davis was right about words casting a spell on you. They certainly did on the rope.

. . . it repeated. Then, in case she missed the message . . .

'Are you serious?' Yen groaned.

But she still began again, ' " One of the stars of the night sky . . ." ' And so on. And On. And ON.

She read it *inside* the Ajax Hotel.

She read it *outside* the Ajax Hotel – by the entrance, behind the wash-house and high up the rickety fire escape.

She'd have read it at roof-level, too – huddled between the chimney pots – except she'd promised never to play there. Instead, just to make a change, she went down to the basement, beyond the room Michael Kwan shared with his granpa, to an old coal-hole dimly lit by a grating in the pavement above.

Yen propped herself beneath it, settled the rope beside her, and opened the book yet again. 'Sky,' she said wearily.

It was as far as she got.

Above her head she heard trip-trapping

footsteps. Next came the creak of the front door. After this, a shrill nagging voice she recognized only too well came echoing down to the coal-hole. 'It's rent day, everyone!'

'Mrs Bagbite,' Yen shuddered.

Every kid in the Ajax Hotel hated rent day. It meant stand-up-straight and hold-your-tongue and don't-let-her-see-that-look-on-your-face. It meant change-those-shoes-at-once-must-you-always-look-so-scruffy? Worst of all, it meant come-here-this-instant-you-need-a-spitwash.

For Mrs Bagbite was worse than a sergeant major.

One slip and she'd pounce. 'There are plenty more where *you* come from,' she'd declare. 'If you can't do better than that, kindly pack your bags and be off!'

The grown-ups were terrified of her. 'She owns the Hotel,' they always said. 'Yes, we know it's dirty and smelly and falling to bits – but where else can we go if she throws us out?'

Mrs Bagbite loved throwing people out.

After she'd collected the rent, of course . . .

She kept it in a leather pouch chained to her wrist with a padlock. Phun reckoned she hid the key up the leg of her knickers. 'It stands to reason,' he said. 'No one would ever –'

'All right,' Yen stopped him. 'That's quite enough, thank you.'

Actually, the slightest mention of Mrs Bagbite was too much for Yen. She preferred to forget her altogether. Maybe today she'd be lucky. Tucked away in the coal-hole, she might miss the whole visit.

Some hopes.

Straight away the dreaded trip-trap of feet rang out on the basement steps, coming closer and closer. The instant she appeared, Mrs Bagbite's eyes narrowed. 'What are you doing there, child?'

'Er . . . nothing, Ma'am.'

'Nothing?'

'Reading, I mean.'

'Reading? In this light?'

Mrs Bagbite peered at her spikily. Everything about her seemed spiky to Yen – her ankles and elbows, her kneecaps and knuckles, even her chin when it wasn't wagging. 'And what is that flickery-dickery thing sitting next to you?' she demanded in a spiky voice.

'My rainbow rope, Ma'am.'

'A rainbow rope? You're reading to a rainbow rope? Don't be ridiculous! You might as well be bathing a bean bag. Rainbow ropes are for *skipping* with. Is that what you're doing – skipping? Indoors? Here at the Ajax Hotel? Disgraceful!'

'No, Ma'am . . .'

'Don't lie to me!'

Yen flinched as bony Bagbite fingers closed over one of her ears. 'Ow!' she yelped.

'Silence!'

Yanking Yen to her feet, Mrs Bagbite sniffed at her with a bony nose. 'There are plenty more where you come from . . .' she began.

It was as far as she got.

Yen had a close-up of spiky eyes glazing over

as the rainbow rope wrapped itself round Mrs Bagbite like a cable round a capstan . . . but a whole lot quicker. In a trice, Mrs Bagbite was trussed up tighter than a Christmas turkey.

It's hard to describe what happened next.

Think of the snap of a whip or the flick that sets off an old-fashioned spinning-top. If this won't do, imagine the jerk that starts an outboard motor . . .

Got it?

That's roughly what the rainbow rope did to Mrs Bagbite. It span her round on the spot till the owner of the Ajax Hotel went wibbly-wobbly, wibbly-wobbly, backwards and forwards across her own basement like . . . well, like the spinning-

top that's just been mentioned. Even after she'd slumped down in a heap, her eyeballs wibble-wobbled on. 'Bag your packs and be off kindly,' she managed to say. 'Er . . . pag your backs and kind off bigly —'

'Can I help, Ma'am?' Yen asked anxiously.

'Nes!'

'Sorry?'

'Yo!'

Yen decided to help her anyway — up the steps, along the hallway and out of the front door. Mrs Bagbite stood there a moment, blinking in the sunlight. 'I'll be bag,' she announced.

'Or pack,' said Yen.

She was trying hard not to giggle as Mrs Bagbite tottered away. Because she *would* be back, definitely. And she'd be bringing trouble with her.

Big Trouble.

Uneasily, Yen watched her out of sight. 'Thanks for sticking up for me, rope,' she said. 'Maybe we really are chums, mates, pals, partners and make-up, make-up, never-never-break-up buddies, et cetera. And I do trust you, honestly. All the same, I can't help thinking you've gone too far this time . . .'

The rainbow rope didn't answer. Well, not really. Yen had seen the word so many times before it didn't seem to count:

was all it said.

After this, like a battery suddenly on the blink, the rope lay still at her feet.

7
Meeting Its Maker

Yen was right about Big Trouble.

Later that day, a sealed envelope was delivered by special messenger to every family at the Ajax Hotel. They guessed at once who had sent it. 'Handwriting as spiky as that?' said Lai and Tran's aunty. 'It's from Mrs Bagbite definitely.'

'She's never written to us before . . .' frowned Michael Kwan's granpa.

'Has she ever missed collecting the rent before? This is serious, I tell you.'

All over the Hotel there was a rustling of paper.

Then silence.

People shook their heads and passed the letter on white-faced. Everyone stared at everyone else with frightened eyes.

The message read:

> NOTICE TO QUIT.
> ALL GUESTS AT THE AJAX HOTEL
> MUST LEAVE BY THE END OF THE
> MONTH. THE HOTEL HAS BEEN SOLD
> AND THE NEW OWNER REQUIRES
> VACANT POSSESSION. THINK
> YOURSELF LUCKY I'VE TOLD YOU
> THIS FAR AHEAD.
> YOURS,
> AGNES BAGBITE.

'Vacant possession?' said Yen. 'What does that mean?'

'It means *empty*,' Phun answered. 'Whoever's bought the Hotel wants all of us out of it.'

'But why?'

'Don't ask me. It doesn't make sense, Yen. I

reckon we haven't got the full story . . .'

Hastily, Yen looked away. How could she explain to Phun that Mrs Bagbite wanted revenge for the incident down in the basement? 'Oh, rope,' Yen sighed.

'Rope?' asked Phun. 'What's your rainbow rope got to do with it?'

'Nothing,' said Yen.

'No?'

Phun eyed her suspiciously.

Not for long, though. He had much more important things to think about now – such as where they might live after the Ajax Hotel had

closed down. Surely the only place left was . . .

No.

Nobody wanted to consider *that*. However tough you were, your mind shied away from the worst fear of all – the fear that kept Granny Po-Po herself awake at night.

WOULD THEY ALL FINISH UP DOWN BY THE RIVER IN CARDBOARD CITY?

Yen took a deep breath and picked up her rope. 'I'm going out for some fresh air,' she gulped.

'Good luck,' said Phun.

She could see he wanted to work the problem out on his computer.

Yen wanted to think, too – about Alice and her amazing adventures through the Looking-Glass, about Sophie in the Land of the Giants, about Hogarth making friends with the Iron Man.

Wouldn't they have known what to do?

Alice, especially.

Alice was the coolest kid Yen had ever come across. Hadn't she coped with human-size insects? Seen off the Lion and Unicorn? Faced down the Red Queen? 'That's who I need to copy,' said Yen. 'Alice is so commonsensical she'd have sorted things out before you can say space-bat-angel-dragon.'

This made her look up as she walked.

High overhead stormclouds were gathering. They looked like galleons in a sunlit ocean.

Yen smiled, wrily. 'Every one of them's burnished with gold,' she said. 'Just like the poem, really. No, rope. Kindly don't write that word – I'm bored to death with it.'

She needn't have worried. The rope over her arm was as dull and droopy as the day after Boxing Day.

Where had its zest gone?

Where had Yen's?

She mooched along the pavement with her face like an upside-down smiley badge. She was thinking about Cardboard City, of course, and what would happen to her dad there. No kid on her way to a kidnap was ever caught more napping than this kid.

'Aaaargh!'

A huge hand clutched at Yen's anorak, lifting her feet almost from the ground. Another hand, just as huge, clamped itself over her mouth. 'Shush, kiddo, shush!'

Half-lifted, half-dragged, she was pulled into an alleyway. 'Shush!' came a third hiss as her captor slipped back the hood of his duffle-coat.

Yen shrunk back in terror.

Then she blinked in surprise.

Hadn't she seen those whiskery ears before? That head as bald as a bollard? Yen fixed him with an Alice-like look. 'You're the shopkeeper who sold me this rope for fifty pence! And you've been following me all week!'

'Not you, kid. It's the rope I've been after. I'm no shopkeeper, either. I *invented* the thing.'

'Invented it?'

'All by myself, yes. I know what you're thinking, kid – that workshop of mine under the railway arch doesn't look up to much, does it?

But it's still where I perfected my masterpiece, this razzle-dazzle rope. There's never been another one like it. Not made of maths and dreams and laser beams the way this one is. Plus a stroke of luck, I admit.'

'Luck, mister?'

'I'm still not sure how it happened – a million-to-one chance, maybe, never to be repeated. For months and months my experiments got nowhere . . . then, one wet and sparkly afternoon there it was on my bench: a rainbow rope with a life of its own! Too much of a life of its own as it turned out. Drove me dotty it did. That's why –'

He broke off, hurriedly.

By now Yen's stare was as hard as Alice's at her toughest. 'That's why you let me have it,' she said. 'Because you found out you couldn't control it. You wanted me to break the rope in, right? The plan was to let me play and play and play with it till it was so worn out you could snatch it back safely. You knew from the start how wild the rope was.'

'Not for much longer, kid.'

'What?'

'It's fading fast, isn't it?'

'Is it?'

'Haven't you noticed?'

Yen hadn't, no.

But she noticed now.

How could she have been so blind? Colourless and slack, the rainbow rope dangled from the crook of her arm with no more oomph than a worn-out washing line. 'What's wrong?' she asked in alarm.

'Nothing's wrong. Who says anything's wrong? Doesn't every rainbow fade in the end? Why should it be different for a rainbow rope? Eventually it just runs out of energy – sooner rather than later with a kid like you setting the pace.'

Yen gaped at the rope in horror. Had she

done this to it? With all her adventures and reading lessons? 'Are you . . . are you saying this is a no-hope rope, mister? That all we can do is watch it die?'

'Not necessarily . . .'

'What then?'

'Simple, kid.'

He lifted a whiskery eyebrow and spread whiskery, inventorish hands to show how trustworthy he was. 'What we do – you and me – is rush this rope straight back to my laboratory under the railway arch for recycling. Good as new, it'll be. Better, in fact, after we've made a few improvements.'

'Improvements?'

'So it's more . . . *manageable*.'

'Tame, you mean,' said Yen.

'Precisely.'

His crocodile smile glittered down at her the way it had done in the workshop. But he kept his hands well away from the rope. Yen didn't miss that. 'It still doesn't like you, does it?' she said.

'What?'

'That's why you daren't come too close – in case the rope hasn't faded enough. You're afraid it doesn't want to be recycled – that it'll give you the same hard time it did before.'

'That's ridiculous!'

'Is it?'

Yen jiggled the rope in her arms. 'Tell him, rope,' she said 'Tell him what *you* want.'

At first there was no response.

Not even a twitch.

Then, stiffly, like a worm unwinding from a winter-long sleep, the rope nudged into its favourite outline:

'There,' said Yen, bundling it up again.

The rainbow rope maker frowned as the first drops of rain began to fall. 'Listen, kid,' he said, 'We're wasting time. Every second counts. Soon we'll have nothing left to recycle. There's money to be made here, can't you see? *Tons* of it. If we're quick and work together we can both be rich.'

'Rich, mister?'

'Certainly! Mass-produced and with proper marketing this rope could earn us a fortune. There's nothing it can't be trained to do – in factories, on television, in schools, on the sportsfield! It's like a high-tech halo without some goody-goody angel to get in the way! Can't you see how keen people will be to buy one? I'll split the profits with you fifty-fifty – straight down the middle. What could be fairer than that? Don't you want to be a millionaire?'

'Not this way,' said Yen sadly.

'Please yourself, then. Who says I still need you? That rope looks feeble enough to me. Give it here . . .'

He stretched out a hand.

'AAARGH!'

Quick as a cobra, the rope had struck.

Its maker reeled back. A livid, rainbow-shaped bruise blazed across his baldness. With the rope already poised for a second strike, he'd missed his chance and he knew it. 'Keep the rope, you little guttersnipe,' he spluttered. 'Just remember my offer when it begins to wither, that's all, as it dwindles bit by bit before your very eyes till it's utterly and totally DEAD. How will you feel then?'

'That's my problem, mister.'

'Your problem? The rope's problem, you mean. That pet of yours is *finished*.'

Spitting with fury, he turned away.

Yen waited till she was sure he had gone. She wasn't in a hurry. Even the rain, falling steadily now in fat glinty blobs, was no bother. 'Ready, rope?' she said. 'I've been pretty dim, I know. But I've finally worked out what to do with you.'

Maybe she imagined the rope's answer. Or maybe it was just dampness in the air. What she heard, though – what, almost certainly, she heard – was a whispery, burp-like sigh of relief.

8

A Pot of Gold

'Wow!' said Yen.

The park on top of the hill dripped with rain.
Yen, on the centre-spot of the football pitch,
dripped too. It was the sky which took her
breath away. It hung so low over the city now
she felt if she stood on tiptoe and stretched –
really stretched – she could dabble her hands in
the blue and grey and the gold of it. 'It's
splendificent!' she murmured. 'It's fantabulous!

It's magnastic!'

What were those words in the poem?

> The sky is simply delicious
> Why haven't I tried it before?
> I can chew my way through to Eternity
> And still have room left for more . . .

Yen grinned at the thought. 'So I don't blame
you, rope,' she said. 'It's not your fault you've
acquired a taste for the cosmos. Me, too, as it
happens.'

Had the rope perked up a bit?

It was certainly more colourful – or was this
just a reflection from overhead?

Yen knelt in the damp grass and laid the rope

over her lap for the last time. 'We didn't skip much, did we rope?' she said. 'We didn't jump much, either, or do anything very much that you're supposed to do with rainbow ropes. Come to think of it, mostly we played a kind of tug-o'-war – with you tugging me step-by-step in the right direction.'

Before she could change her mind, she stood up.

She dried her hands carefully on her hanky so her grip would be firm. Then she took hold of the rope at one end. 'Prepare for take-off!' she said.

WIRRA-WIRRA-WIRRA went the rainbow rope as she whirled it faster and faster round her head.

Soon it was as blurry as the blades of a helicopter. Yen's feet nearly left the ground. The whole park seemed to tremble under her.

That's when she let go.

SWISH!

Had she thrown hard enough?

The rainbow rope soared into the sky as if it belonged there. It seemed to split, to spread, to arch across clouds and no-clouds from one side of the world to the other.

Yen gaped at it, her mouth rounded for the

biggest WOW of all. She couldn't say even that because what happened next out-wowed her altogether along with everyone else in the city who happened to be looking up at that moment.

Using the sky as a scribbling pad and the horizon for a guideline, the rope wrote out its last word. Each letter unfolded in a sweeping, multicoloured scrawl.

. . . is what it said.

NEVER BEFORE OR SINCE – AND FEEL FREE TO CHECK THE RECORD BOOKS – HAS A RAINBOW SPELLED SOMEONE'S NAME.

Alone on the hilltop, Yen blushed with pride as she waved goodbye.

'You were FUN while you lasted, rope,' she called. 'Worth all of fifty pence. I'll never have a better birthday present as long as I live!'

Then she pulled her skimpy anorak around her, patted the empty pocket of her worn-out jeans and forced herself not to feel lonely as she plodded back the way she'd come.

At this point you'd better stop reading . . .

No, the story isn't quite over.

It's just that the next bit – the last bit of all – is so daft, so dickory, so ding-dong, curly-whirly, cuckoo-boingumptious it's even more incredible than everything so far. Only someone like Yen – or maybe a kid who could easily be her very best friend – would even *try* to believe it.

So shut the book now, please.

Be *sensible*.

No?

Serves you right, then. Some people are so stubborn they'll believe anything, even the truth.

For when Yen reached the corner of the dead-end street she'd be leaving any day now, she stopped in her tracks. 'What's going on?' she said faintly.

Why were her mum and dad dancing up and down the steps of the Ajax Hotel? Why was Granny Po-Po hugging Michael's granpa – while Lai and Tran's uncle and aunty swapped kisses with Anh and Susoi's mum and dad? Why was her big brother Johnny playing leapfrog across the pavement with her little brother Phun and all the other kids? 'Is it a party?' asked Yen, running up.

'Why not?' Johnny laughed. 'With a change

of luck like this I'll be a car mechanic by this time next year!'

'And I'll be fit for a job!' beamed her dad.

'Luck?' said Yen. 'What luck?'

'We're moving!' Phun explained. 'I *knew* that letter of Mrs Bagbite didn't give the whole picture, Yen! Can you guess who's bought the Ajax Hotel? It's the City Council! We've just had a visitor from the housing department who told us this place is so slummy they want to pull it down altogether. That's why we've got to get out. They're offering us proper homes instead – on a brand-new estate out at the city limits!'

'Where the country begins?' Yen gasped.

'That's right!'

Yen felt so dizzy with happiness she had to hold Phun's arm to stay upright. 'It's just like a story,' she said. 'It's like Story Number Five to add to my Favourite Four – except it's *my* story! And it's actually happening! It's happening to us!'

Quickly, she looked at the sky.

She could barely see the rainbow now. It had faded into the blue the way all rainbows do in the end. Anyway, what possible link could there be between a rainbow rope – even one made of maths and dreams and laser beams – and her family finding its fortune at last?

Was this her pot of gold?

Yen giggled and shook her head. 'Even I can't quite believe that,' she said. 'Not in a million, trillion years!'

But she still whispered thank you, just in case.

Dear Reader,

        If you'd like to read for
yourself the Favourite Four books I talk
about in this story, here are the details :-

THROUGH THE LOOKING-GLASS
                        by Lewis Carroll
(Puffin Classics isbn 0 14 035.039 x)

THE IRON MAN by Ted Hughes
(Faber and Faber isbn 0571 141 498)

THE BFG by Roald Dahl
(Puffin isbn 0 14 03.1597 7)

SKY IN THE PIE by Roger McGough
(Puffin isbn 0 14 03.1612 4)

I hope you enjoy them . Of course, maybe
you've got a Favourite Four of your own...
or maybe five or six or seven even. If you
agree with me that a book can be just as
much fun as a razzle-dazzle rainbow
then count yourself a friend of mine !

                        Love from
                        Yen.

Acknowledgements

The Iron Man by Ted Hughes, © copyright, Ted Hughes by kind permission of Faber & Faber Ltd; 'The Sky in the Pie' by Roger McGough, reprinted from *Sky in the Pie* by Roger McGough (Kestrel Books, 1983) by permission of Peters Fraser & Dunlop.